D0226796

# Mr Birdsnest
## and the House
# Next Door

# Mr Birdsnest
## and the House
# Next Door

### Julia Donaldson

Illustrated by
**Hannah Shaw**

Barrington Stoke

First published in 2012 in Great Britain by
Barrington Stoke Ltd
18 Walker Street, Edinburgh, EH3 7LP

www.barringtonstoke.co.uk

This edition first published 2016

Text © 2012 Julia Donaldson
Illustrations © 2012 Hannah Shaw

Colouring by Catriona Black

The moral right of Julia Donaldson and Hannah Shaw to be
identified as the author and illustrator of this work has been
asserted in accordance with the Copyright, Designs and
Patents Act, 1988

All rights reserved. No part of this publication may be
reproduced in whole or in any part in any form without the
written permission of the publisher

A CIP catalogue record for this book is available
from the British Library upon request

ISBN: 978-1-78112-575-5

Printed in China by Leo

This book is super readable for young readers beginning
their independent reading journey.

*To everyone at Miltonbank Primary School*

# Contents

# Chapter 1
## Mr Crocodile

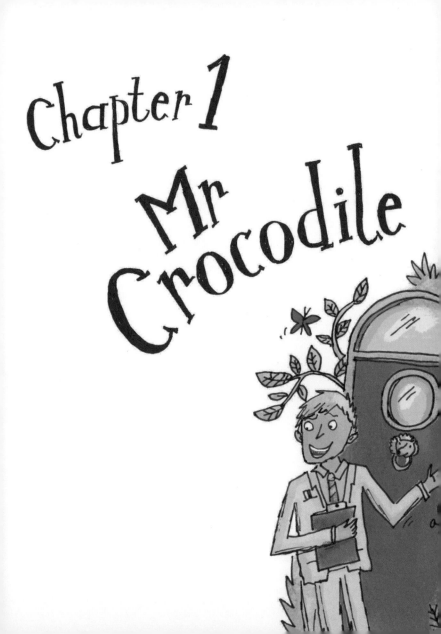

When Dad told us Granny was going to come and live with us, my little brother Elmo said, "There's no room. Is she going to sleep in the bath?"

"No, she'll need her own bedroom," said Dad. "We're going to have to look for a new house."

Granny couldn't live on her own
any more because she kept getting into
muddles. She had a black cat called
Panther, and sometimes she put dry cat
food instead of cat litter into the tray
where he did his poos.

Panther didn't mind – he just ate the food.  But he did mind the day Granny put cat litter in his bowl instead of cat food.

Mum and Dad were worried that Granny might feed herself the wrong things, or leave the oven on, or forget to turn the tap off.

We went to look at a lot of houses. The man who showed us the houses was called Mr Mills, but Elmo called him Mr Crocodile. When I asked why he said it was "because of his big false toothy smile".

"Do you mean he has false teeth or a false smile?" I asked.

"Both," Elmo said.

Most of the houses we looked at had something wrong with them.  But Mr Crocodile just smiled and said they were "charming".

Then one day Mr Crocodile took us to see an empty house. The path up to the door had thick bushes growing over it. Butterflies were fluttering about.

"This will be charming once the garden's all cut back," said Mr Crocodile. But Elmo and I liked it the way it was.

The front door of the house had a lovely knocker in the shape of a lion's head.

Inside it was all empty and bare, and there were a lot of cobwebs. Mum and Dad walked around slowly with Mr Crocodile, but Elmo and I raced about. We ran up the clattery stairs, and looked in all the rooms and cupboards.

One of the bedrooms had wallpaper with jungle plants and monkeys on it. There was a big cupboard, the kind you can walk right into.

Inside the cupboard there was an enormous spider's web with a big fat spider sitting on it.

"Maybe it's a bird-eating spider," said Elmo.

When Mr Crocodile and Mum and Dad came upstairs, Elmo and I raced up to them.

"We've got to buy this house!" I said.

"It's got butterflies and a lion and monkeys and a bird-eating spider," said Elmo. "It's a jungle house!"

Mum and Dad didn't look too sure, even when Elmo said he'd give them some of his pocket money to help pay for it. They said the bedroom downstairs was too small and dark for Granny.

"Mr Mills says the house next door is for sale too," said Mum. "Let's go and have a look at that."

The lady who lived in the house next door didn't look very happy when she saw Elmo and me. She made us take our shoes off before she let us in.

We followed the grown-ups round all the boring rooms. Most of them had wallpaper with flowers on. There was a smell like flowers too. I think it was all the polish the lady put on her tables and chairs.

When we left, Elmo said, "That was a horrible flowerpot house! We can't move there! If we do, I'll run away."

But Mum and Dad liked it.

"That sunny bedroom would be just right for Granny," Dad said.

In the end we did move to the flowerpot house. Mum, Dad and Granny liked it, but it didn't feel like home to Elmo and me. Elmo hated the flowers on the wallpaper in his room.

He made up a song –

"Roses are red, violets are blue,
Flush the lot of them down the loo."

After three days of that, Dad told
Elmo to get lost.

"All right," said Elmo, "I will."

And the next thing we knew, he was
gone.

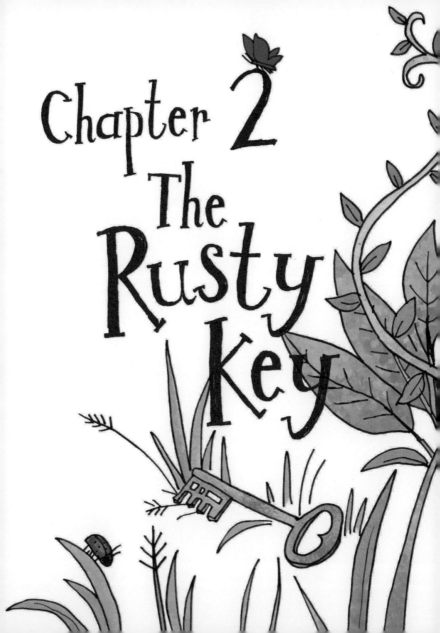

# Chapter 2
# The Rusty Key

We looked all over the house and garden for Elmo. We even drove to our old house in case he had gone back there, but he hadn't. We started to get really worried then, and Mum rang the police.

While we were waiting for the police to come I had an idea.

There was still no one in the jungle
house next door. I went out into our
garden and climbed over the wall.

The grass in the jungle garden was long and swishy, not like the short neat grass in our garden. I stood still and listened.

There was a sound from inside one of the bushes, and out jumped Panther. He went over to a tall thick tree and I followed him.  The tree looked very old, and there was a big hole in the trunk, like a door.  I looked inside.

There in the tree, curled up and fast asleep, was Elmo.

After that we went to play in the garden of the jungle house every day. Sometimes Panther came with us. He chased insects and leaves. We pretended he was a real panther in a real jungle.

One day, Panther was chasing some leaves under the old tree when I noticed something metal in the grass. It was an old key.

"Maybe it fits the back door of the jungle house," I said.

We tried it in the key hole, and it did!

The door opened with a creak, and we went inside.

The jungle house looked just like the last time we'd seen it, but now there were more cobwebs.

The spider in the cupboard in the monkey bedroom looked even fatter than before. "That spider must have eaten a lot of birds," said Elmo.

We played on the stairs for a while.

"I wish we lived here," I said.

"Well, we can," said Elmo. "No one else lives here, and we've got the key."

We came back the next day and the day after. We made a den in the cupboard in the monkey bedroom.

We took some polish from our house and polished the lion door knocker till it shone.  But we didn't clean anything else. We wanted the jungle house to stay full of cobwebs and secrets.

One day we let Panther in. We wanted him to meet the bird-eating spider. They were just saying hello when we heard the front door open.

I grabbed Panther. Elmo shut the door of the cupboard and we kept very quiet.

We could hear footsteps on the stairs. Two men were talking. One of them was Mr Crocodile. He kept saying, "Charming." The other man's voice was low and mumbly. He kept saying, "Yes, yes ..."

The footsteps came into the room. They came right up to the cupboard. Then the door handle started to turn!

We pressed ourselves up against the wall behind the door. But Mr Crocodile only opened the door a tiny bit.

He said, "Another good cupboard," and the other man said, "Perfect."

The footsteps were going away again when something awful happened. Panther jumped out of my arms! He landed on the floor with a thud.

"Do we have a ghost?" the mumbly voice said.

The next moment Mr Crocodile had opened the cupboard door again and found us.

# Chapter 3

# Mr Birdsnest

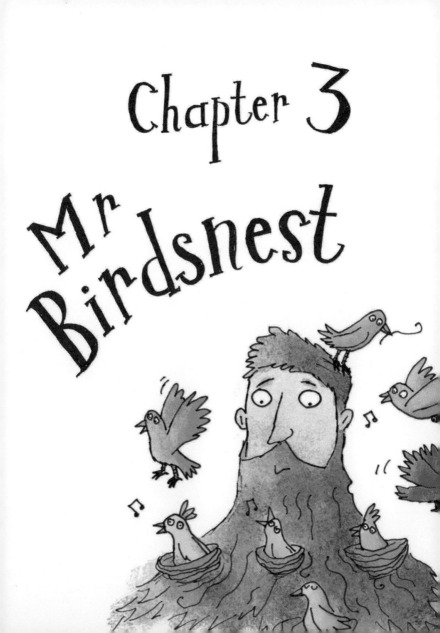

Mr Crocodile was very angry. For once he didn't even smile. The other man said, "Three ghosts." He had a white face and a long grey beard and we couldn't tell if he was angry or not.

Mr Crocodile made us give him the key and then he took us back to the flowerpot house. Dad said we weren't to play next door again – not even in the garden.

"Why not?" Elmo said. "No one lives there."

"That man is going to buy it," said Dad. "He won't want you playing there."

"He must be a very greedy man if he wants the whole jungle house all for himself," I said.

Elmo said maybe the man had a lot of birds' nests in his beard and so he needed some rooms for the birds to fly around in. Mum told him not to be silly, but I laughed. After that we called the man Mr Birdsnest.

We missed playing in the jungle garden a lot. Mum and Dad had started to make a pond in our garden, but it wasn't finished yet. Elmo and I kept looking over the wall at the hollow tree next door.

"Mean old Mr Birdsnest," said Elmo.

A few weeks later, a big van stopped outside the jungle house.

Elmo and I looked out of the window and saw some men lift out all Mr Birdsnest's things. He had a great long table which was covered in blankets. It looked too big for one man.

"Greedy old Mr Birdsnest!" said Elmo.
"He must need an enormous table for his
enormous dinners."

"Look at all those boxes," I said.
"They're all covered with blankets too.
What do you think is in them?"

"I bet it's the Crown Jewels," said Elmo.

Even though we weren't allowed to go in the jungle garden any more, no one could stop Panther playing there. The day after Mr Birdsnest moved in, Panther was sitting under the hollow tree when the back door of the jungle house opened and a huge stripy cat ran out and jumped on him. Panther raced back into our garden.

"Mr Birdsnest's got a tiger!" said Elmo.

Then out came Mr Birdsnest himself.
He had a saw and he started sawing
some thin branches off the hollow tree.

"Oh no!" I said.  "He's going to cut it
down!"

"He's evil," said Elmo.

The next day we were in our garden when Elmo shouted, "Look!" and pointed to a window of the jungle house. Someone was standing with their back to the window. It looked like Granny.

"Mr Birdsnest has kidnapped her!" said Elmo.

We ran in to tell Mum and Dad.  They were busy putting dinosaur wallpaper up in Elmo's room.  Mum told us not to be so silly.  She said that Granny was out posting a letter.  It must be someone else at the window.

But when we went back into the garden and looked up again, the person turned round, and it was Granny. What's more, she was waving to us.

"She wants us to come and save her," I said.

# Chapter 4
## The Rescue

How could we get to Granny? We didn't
have the key to the jungle house any
more.

"Perhaps the back door is open," I
said.

We climbed over the wall and ran to the back door of the jungle house. I turned the handle. The door opened.

"Let's leave it open in case we have to run for it," I said in a whisper.

We had often been in the jungle
house before, but this time it felt scary.
I could feel my heart thump as we crept
through the kitchen.

As soon as we opened the door from the kitchen into the hall we heard a noise. It was a twittering, squawking noise.

"It's Mr Birdsnest's birds!" said Elmo.

It was true, the noise did sound like a lot of birds. It was coming from one of the downstairs rooms.

Elmo and I sneaked past and crept up the stairs.

When we got to the monkey bedroom we heard a clunking sound.

"What's that?" I whispered.

Then there was another sound. It was louder, like a heavy ball falling.

"What is Granny doing in there?" said Elmo. "Is she locked in?"

I turned the door handle.  The door opened.

There stood Granny, with a long stick in her hands.  She was pointing it at a white ball which was sitting on top of a big long table.

And standing next to Granny, with another stick, was Mr Birdsnest!

"Ooh, you made me jump," said Granny.

"Well, well, it's those ghosts again," said Mr Birdsnest.

We had planned to run if we saw him, but it didn't seem right now. Mr Birdsnest had a big smile on his face, and so did Granny.

"I hope you don't mind me borrowing your grandmother," said Mr Birdsnest. "I found her on my doorstep."

Granny must have got into one of her muddles on the way back from the post box and gone to the wrong house.

"I asked her in for a cup of tea and a game of snooker," said Mr Birdsnest. "And now she's beating me."

Just then Granny got the black ball down a hole, which meant she had won. Good old Granny! I never even knew she could play snooker.

"Now," said Mr Birdsnest, "do you want to meet my friends, children?"

He took us down to the room where we'd heard all the twittering and squawking.

When he opened the door we saw a sheet of wire netting. It stretched from the floor to the ceiling. Behind the netting were lots and lots of bright coloured birds. Some were flapping about and some were sitting on the branches Mr Birdsnest had cut off the tree in the garden.

Elmo and I stared and stared. Then Elmo said, "Did you bring them all here in your beard?"

Mr Birdsnest laughed and said he'd brought them in cages covered with blankets.

"So it wasn't the Crown Jewels," I said.

"You'd better not let the bird-eating spider get your birds!" Elmo said.

Mr Birdsnest said it was all right. He had put the spider out in the garden where it was quite happy eating flies.

After that we were all friends, except for Tiger and Panther. They seemed to like being enemies.

Mr Birdsnest didn't cut the old tree down. Instead, he built a den in the branches for me and Elmo. It had a door and a window, and a rope ladder to climb up to it.

So now we have our own jungle house. It doesn't have monkey wallpaper of course, but when Mr Birdsnest found out how much we liked the lion door knocker he took it off his own front door and put it onto the tree house one.

"That's in case your grandmother ever comes to visit," he said.

Our books are tested
for children and young people by
children and young people.

Thanks to everyone who consulted on
a manuscript for their time and effort in
helping us to make our books better
for our readers.

Little
Gems

NOW IN COLOUR

From the author of *The Gruffalo!*

The
Snake
Who Came
to Stay

Julia
Donaldson

Illustrated by Hannah Shaw

ANNA
LIZA
and the
Happy
Practice

CHILDREN'S
LAUREATE
IRELAND
2014–2016

EOIN COLFER
Illustrated by Matt Robertson